Hi I'm Feely and this is my diary.

There are six Feely books so far. It's best to read them in this order:

1   Feely's Magic Diary

2   Feely for Prime Minister

3   Feely and Her Well-Mad Parents

4   Feely Goes to Work

5   Feely and Henry VIII

6   Feely and Someone Else's Granny

Feely and Henry VIII
by Barbara Catchpole
Illustrated by Jan Dolby

Published by Ransom Publishing Ltd.
Unit 7, Brocklands Farm, West Meon, Hampshire GU32 IJN, UK
www.ransom.co.uk

ISBN   978 1785911255
First published in 2016

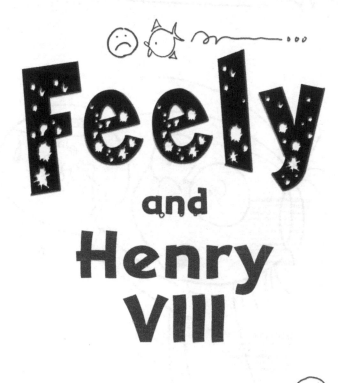

Feely

and

Henry

VIII

Barbara Catchpole

Illustrated by Jan Dolby

Ransom

Thursday

Dear Diary

I love half terms! What I really want to do

is lie in bed until late (not as late as Ollie,

my smelly brother), read loads and hang

around the shops a bit with my mates

from the Drama Club.

Drama
Club

Sometimes, if I can, I play on the Wii,

but not often. Usually Ollie and his huge

mates are lying about in the lounge with

some legs and arms and maybe the odd

bottom sticking out into the hall.

Talking of bottoms, why

don't they buy jeans that pull up properly?

I don't need to see that!

There's loads of trainers in the hall

smelling bad, as well.
You can see
little curls of
smell come off
them, like in
cartoons.

Half terms are good because Dad doesn't
try to teach us anything. He's a teacher –
it's not just what he does, it's what he *is*

He likes to tell people about stuff.
Anybody. Like he talks to random kids
about dirty old kettles in museums.

One little girl started to cry when he
told her about Henry VIII chopping off his

wives' heads and her mother told Dad off
and reported him to the museum guy. Dad
got told to leave people alone.

Thankfully half terms are too short for
him to get round to spoiling things for us.

First he does his marking after
wandering around the house in his pants
looking for a red pen.

('There must be one somewhere. Where do things go in this house? Is there a black hole sucking in all my stuff? Do you know about black  holes? I'll get dressed after I find my red pen, Susan, thank you! Why is it in the bathroom? For the love of Mike!')

I bet you didn't think teachers wander round in their pants! Well, yes they do! Sometimes even the Homer Simpson ones he got for Father's Day.

Then he gets his lessons ready ('I don't know why the kids don't find Shakespeare interesting. Come and listen to the poetry, Feely! Did you know Shakespeare ... blah ... blah ... blaaaaah).

Then he has an hour off and half term's over.

He's supposed to look after us, but

really he just yells
through the door of
his room:

'You kids still
out there?'

every now and
again, and

'Anyone want to bring me a coke?
Anyone? Anyone?'

This half term was different, though. Miss
Rosy had forgotten that Henry, our class
goldfish, needed looking after and she was
going away for the week.

'When was she going to do her marking

and her lesson prep?' I hear you ask. Well, Diary, she probably doesn't do any. She's fairly useless.

Mum says she doesn't look any older than I do.

So on the last day before half term Miss Rosy clapped her hands three times for silence and we all carried on talking like we usually do.

'Class! Class! Shane! Put it down! Now! Not on Stacey's head! I have a huge thing to ask you. Henry, our goldfish, needs looking after at half term. He's been a bit poorly so I don't like to leave him alone here. Now he's a very interesting little chap.'

(Miss Rosy picked up the fishbowl. Henry really wasn't interesting. He'd have to work hard to be boring. He was just nothing, really.)

'And quite clever.'

(The rock in his bowl was cleverer than Henry.)

'I am sure you would learn loads and loads of amazing, awesome stuff about goldfish!'

(I was sure I wouldn't.)

'So who will take him home? Come on,
fifty merit points!'   FISH ......

Saffron's hand shot up, of course.

I can't stand her and her nasty little gang.

She might as well

just leave her

hand in the air, it

goes up that

many times a

day. Or have a

fake one sewn

onto the shoulder

of her blouse,

pointing straight up.

So I put my hand up as well, just to

annoy her. (Also I could do with a few merit points)

Just as Miss Rosy turned back towards us, Saffron yanked my hand down and Miss Rosy saw it!

'Saffron, don't do that! We are all friends in this class and we are kind to one another. Fiona, you can take Henry home.'

'My name is Phoebe, Miss. Thank you, Miss.'

She's taught me for weeks and she doesn't know my name. My proper name is Phoebe but I'm Feely to people I like — and that's you, dear Diary, and the Drama Club!

Saffron was gutted:

'I don't think I could have had him anyway, Feely. Mummy might take me skiing and of course I've got my

pony to look after. Did I tell you I've got my own pony?

'Are you sure you want to do it, though? Don't breathe over the bowl because your toilet breath will probably kill him.

'Miss! I don't think Feely should have him, Miss. She's got bad breath, Miss. He'll die and we will all be upset and cry, Miss. My mum will come up the school. Feely can't do anything right, Miss. Miss!'

18

'Don't be silly, Saffron,' Miss Rosy said. (She knows everyone else's name – what's wrong with mine?) 'But he is very old in fish years. Very old indeed.'

Oh great! Now Henry was going to pass away to the Great Goldfish Bowl in the Sky and I was going to be a Fish Murderer and everyone would hate me.

Stress on a stick!

fish

Friday

I can't tell you how pleased Mum was that I was taking the goldfish home today. I can't tell you that because she wasn't pleased at all. <u>FISH</u>..... 🐟

'Good God, Feely! Haven't I got enough to do without having to baby sit a goldfish. Look at it! It's on its last legs!'

I know, I know –
but I didn't say
anything about the
legs – she was narky
enough as it was.

'Don't Mum! Saffron said I would kill him!
The whole class will hate me if he dies!'

Mum looked round at me (and almost
hit a traffic island – she is a terrible
driver).

'I promise you he won't die, Feely. It's
OK.'

We drove home at ten miles an hour with
other cars honking at us all the way. The

water slopped out of the bowl every time
we went around a corner and after the
speed bumps in our road
there was only an
inch or two in the
bowl. Henry had to
lie sideways at the
bottom.

By the time we put him in Dad's study,
Henry was very fed up. Dad said:

'I don't want that thing in here!'

'Well it's going in here where it's cool'

I sloshed some more water in Henry's
bowl – I put some in from the hot tap to

give him a bit of a warm bath.

After that he was doing a bit of a fancy stroke, lying on his side again, so I thought he must be happy.

Mum and I were watching a Harry Potter film and eating popcorn which she had burned for me, when Ollie shouted,

'Henry's dead!'

Dad had gone out somewhere all of a sudden before the film, so Mum went and had a look.

I couldn't bear it. My heart thumped

and I just tried to will him to be alive.

'Just sleeping!' Mum shouted to me. 'Just having a little fish nap – like a cat nap, only wetter!'

'But ... but ... ' Ollie said.

'Go to bed, Ollie! *Now* ! *Do as I say!*'

Mum was really ratty. I guess she had been a bit worried about Henry too. Thank goodness he was OK!

Saturday

Oh Diary, I am so clumsy! This morning Henry looked great. He was swimming around like a loony and he even looked like he had grown a bit.

But there were loads of little goldfish poos floating about in the water. Mum was in the garden chopping down some poor bush and yakking to old Mrs Jones.

'I'll sort him out later!' she said.

Well, I thought, I wouldn't like to be

swimming about in my own poo. So I took him into the kitchen, very carefully. No, I didn't drop him!

I used the tea strainer to get him out and I put him in a cup of water. No, again! All fine!

So I cleaned out the bowl and I gave him fresh water and I even gave his little plastic castle a bit of a wash with washing up liquid. But when I went to pour him back in – he was gone! He had jumped out!

I looked on the floor – gone! Then I saw him – stuck down the side of the washing machine. I got him out with a spoon.

He was covered in that fluffy dust.

Then he jumped off! I picked him up in my hands and rinsed him under the tap, but then I dropped him again! He was lying gasping in the sink. His little mouth was opening and closing really fast.

Should I give him the kiss of life? I wondered.

Ommmmmmm... ....

'Feely! Put him back in the water, doofus!' Ollie came in and picked him up by his tail and dropped him back in the bowl.

Henry just sank to the bottom and lay there, not moving at all. There were loads of bubbles in the bowl. I can't have rinsed the plastic castle off properly.

'What have I done?' I cried out. 'Mum!'

'Dead as a dead thing!' said Ollie, 'Burial at sea – can I flush him away?'

'Just resting!' said Mum. 'Just having a little nap after his walk.' (I know, but I was too upset to say)

She picked up the bowl and ran off with it.

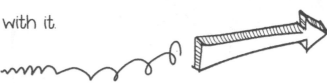

Sunday

This morning Henry was swimming about, quite happy. He had gone a bit lighter, but I thought probably that was because of the washing up liquid making him a bit cleaner.

I put loads of food in for him and I think he ate too much, because he was swimming around upside-down.

Mum had to rush off with him again to give him a bit of a lie down! I don't think she understands how goldfish work!

Monday

Again, this morning, quite happy! He's gone a bit more orange. I expect he's getting a bit dirtier again.

I gave him some of the yummy cheesecake I had for dinner and that slowed him down.

Tuesday

Left Henry on the side in the kitchen today to warm up. Mum was quite cross. She said that's why they call them *coldwater fish* and could I please just leave him alone!

Wednesday

Ollie said Henry looked a bit 'green about

the gills' this evening

and Mum said Ollie had

better think very

carefully before he

gave us any more

Fish Health Reports.

She said it was true Henry looked better

in the mornings, but perhaps he was a

Morning Person – or at least a Morning

Fish.

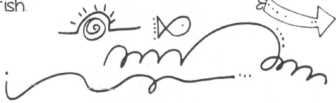

Thursday

Ollie said he was eating Henry for lunch today! Turns out it was only those fish-shaped fish finger things.

He told me quite a funny goldfish joke:

A little boy is digging a big hole and the bloke next door asks him what he is doing. The little boy says he is burying his dead goldfish.

Then the bloke asks:

'Why are you digging such a big hole?'

'Because it's inside your cat!'

Well, I thought it was funny. ☺

I don't like cats much. Next door's cat thinks our garden is one big toilet.

I didn't spend so much time with Henry

today because I thought Stick, our stick
insect, might be dead. ☹

Then I realised I had been watching a
real stick by mistake and Stick was OK and
hanging onto the lid.

Pets are very stressful.

↪pets

Friday

Never put fish in a blender! Let me tell you

what happened. I'm only just getting over it!

Well Henry was swimming about,

well-happy like he does in the mornings.

He had a little trail of poo coming out

of him and he was whizzing round the tank.

He was saying, 'Bob. Bob, Bob!'

Mum had gone out to the shops and couldn't stop me, so I decided to give him a clean out. No washing up liquid!

Dad explained (for twenty-three minutes — I timed him) why that was bad. No hot water! (Eighteen minutes, but he only stopped because the news came on)

I wasn't going to put him in a cup he could jump out of, either.

There was a plastic jug with a top on it on the side in the kitchen. I had seen it before, but I couldn't remember what it was for!

I put him in there. Then the phone went. It was Hannah asking how Henry was. I was just in the hall talking to her when I heard Ollie shout out from the kitchen:

'I'm gonna use the blender, Feely!'

Why would I care?

'Using it now, Feely!'

What was he on about? Wait a minute

— the blender! For turning things to mush!

The plastic jug!

Nooooooooooooooooo!!

As I ran into the kitchen, Ollie was just

standing with his finger on the switch.

'No!' I shouted. 'No! Henry's in there!'

'Sorry – can't hear you!' he said, and switched it on. It made that horrible blender noise and the plastic jug turned orange! He just laughed!

I just stood there and then I started to cry. Big drops were falling from my face. It was a proper can't-get-your-breath never-gonna-stop cry!

Ollie was laughing fit to bust, but when I carried on crying and was really upset, he told me it was only carrots in there. He had put Henry in the washing up bowl.

'Honestly, Feely, did you think goldfish were orange all the way through? You are so dumb!'

Saturday Night

I bet you haven't guessed this! Mum and Dad have been lying to me! They tell me never to lie, but they are Big Fat Lying Liars!

I was having a bit of a row with Ollie about my toothbrush – he took mine because he had used his to clean his trainers (dog poo again). Mum didn't have

another brush, so he used my toothbrush –

gross!

I was really fed up with him. I was going

to tell Mum about the Curious Incident of

the Fish in the Blender. I'd tell Dad as well!

I called him a thief and he said I was a fish

murderer.

'Every day, you kill a fish and every

night they put a new one in,' said Ollie.

You've killed seven – I've been counting.

You are a serial killer!'

It wasn't

true, was it?

Then I

thought about it.

At night Henry

looked poorly. In

the morning he

looked like new.

That night I cried myself to sleep.

Sunday

Next morning my eyes were all red and sore. I went to see Henry VIII and just sat looking at him. I was a bad person.

'Feely, love, whatever is the matter?' Mum put her arm around me.

'I killed all those fish!'

I was crying now, big salt drops falling into the bowl. Mum moved it away quickly.

'Oh no, Feely, who told you that? Oh, I know — Ollie! He is SO grounded! I'm taking the plug off his computer again — for months this  time, maybe a year! No, love, they are OK — come and see!'

And in the spare room was a huge tank with loads of goldfish, all looking almost the same, swimming around in loads of bubbles with plants and a little Spongebob Squarepants to play with.

It was Fish Paradise!

'You see, Feely, goldfish don't do well in bowls,' Dad said. 'It's to do with the oxygen ... blah di blah ... '.

Nineteen minutes later, Mum said, 'So every night we swopped them over so they could have a rest from the bowl and ... er

... you looking after them.
So they could get back
on their feet.'

I know! No feet!

'But why have we got
so many?'

My favourite is Henry VIII. He's got a
black spot on his mouth.

'Um ... because Dad bought some
spares.'

So *they* didn't think I could look after a
fish either! Still ... just as well.

Monday

Back at school — yeuch!

I told Dad we couldn't keep any Henry in the bowl any more if they didn't like it.

Mum made Dad give the tank and the air thingy and the plants and the Spongebob Squarepants to the school.

('But it cost me nearly a hundred and fifty quid, Susan. Goldfish don't grow on trees.')

I told Miss Rosy it was because I liked

my class so much and she gave me a

hundred merits.

Saffron even looked to see if she could

see Henry the First. There he was –

waving a fin at her.

'Well, there's Henry!' Saffron said, 'but

I still think it's a bit fishy!'

She was right – it was a very fishy story! But at least it didn't end in a burial at sea.

Or down the loo.

fish

...Drama Club...

About the author

Barbara Catchpole was a teacher for thirty years and enjoyed every minute. She has three sons of her own who were always perfectly behaved and never gave her a second of worry.

Barbara also tells lies.

How many have you read?

How many have you read?

Have you met ?

Meet P.I.G - Peter Ian Green, although everybody calls him PIG for short. PIG lives with his mum.

He is small for his age, but says his mum is huge for hers. She is a single mum, but PIG says she looks more like a double mum or even a treble mum.

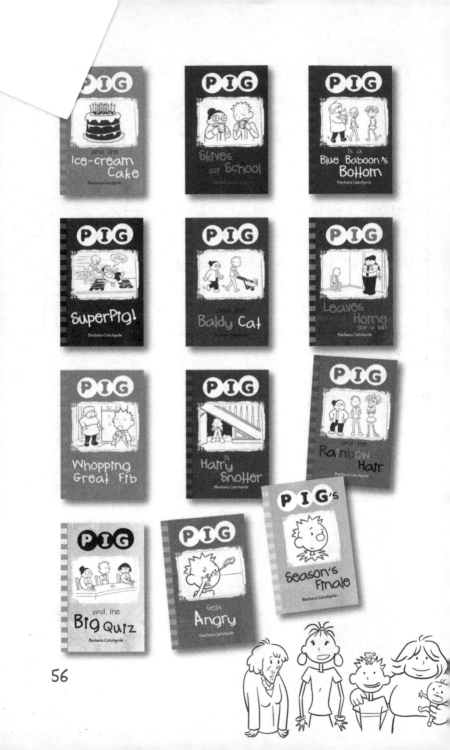